EARLY BIRD
STORIES™

The Black and White Club

Early ★ Reader

First American edition published in 2019 by Lerner Publishing Group, Inc.

An original concept by Alice Hemming
Copyright © 2020 Alice Hemming

Illustrated by Kimberley Scott

First published by Maverick Arts Publishing Limited

Maverick
arts publishing

Licensed Edition
The Black and White Club

Lerner Publications Company
A division of Lerner Publishing Group, Inc.
241 First Avenue North
Minneapolis, MN 55401 USA

For reading levels and more information, look up this title at www.lernerbooks.com.

Main body text set in Mikado. Typeface provided by HVD Fonts.

Library of Congress Cataloging-in-Publication Data

Names: Hemming, Alice, author. | Scott, Kimberley, illustrator.
Title: The black and white club / by Alice Hemming ; illustrated by Kimberley Scott.
Description: Minneapolis : Lerner Publications, [2019] | Series: Early bird readers. Orange (Early bird stories) | "The original picture book text for this story has been modified by the author to be an early reader." | Originally published in Horsham, West Sussex by Maverick Arts Publishing Ltd. in 2015.
Identifiers: LCCN 2018043764 (print) | LCCN 2018052755 (ebook) | ISBN 9781541561700 (eb pdf) | ISBN 9781541542082 (lb : alk. paper)
Subjects: LCSH: Readers (Primary) | Zoo animals—Juvenile literature. | Belonging (Social psychology)—Juvenile literature.
Classification: LCC PE1119 (ebook) | LCC PE1119 .H4767 2019 (print) | DDC 428.6/2—dc23

LC record available at https://lccn.loc.gov/2018043764

Manufactured in the United States of America
1-45393-39009-11/12/2018

EARLY BIRD STORIES

The Black and White Club

Alice Hemming

Illustrated by
Kimberley Scott

Lerner Publications ◆ Minneapolis

It was a quiet evening at the
wildlife park.

Suddenly, George the giraffe saw some animals creeping past.

"Where are you going?"

George asked his best friend, Sid.

"To the Black and White Club," said Sid.

"That sounds fun," said George.

The penguins ran the club.

"Can I join?" said George.

"No," said the penguins.

"You are not black and white."

But they let Sid in.

All the other animals kept
talking about the club.

George felt sad.

George tried to get in the back door.

It did not work.

He painted himself black and white.

That did not work, either.

George tried to make a club
for giraffes . . . but he was the
only giraffe.

Then he made the Yellow With Brown Spots Club . . . but it was a very small club.

So George started the

Tall and Short Club.

They wrote a long list of rules.

They made badges.

Everyone wanted to join the club!

"Can I join?" asked Toni the elephant.

"Yes!" said George.

"Can I join?" asked Minnie the mouse.

"All right, then," said George.

"Can I join?" asked Gus the hippo.

George was not sure.

Gus was not tall or short.

"I'm tall this way," said Gus.

He stretched out his arms very wide.

"OK!" said George.

Mo the flamingo and Max the chimp were medium-sized.

"Well, I'm taller than him," said Mo.

"And I'm shorter than her," said Max.

"OK!" said George.

"Can I be in two clubs?" asked Sid.

"Of course you can!" said George.

Soon, all the animals at the
park joined the club.

The Tall and Short Club
was a lot of fun.

Only the penguins did not want to join in.

They would rather play with dominoes!

Quiz

1. What is the name of George's best friend?
   a) Sam
   b) Steve
   c) Sid

2. What do the penguins like playing with?
   a) Cards
   b) Dominoes
   c) Yo-yos

3. What size is Toni the Elephant?
   a) Medium
   b) Big
   c) Small

4. What type of animal is Minnie?
   a) A mouse
   b) A frog
   c) A bird

5. Why can't George join the penguins' club?
   a) He isn't a penguin.
   b) He isn't black or white.
   c) He is too tall.

EARLY BIRD
STORIES

COLOR		GRL
Purple		J-K
Orange		H-J
Green		G-I
Blue		E-G
Yellow		C-E
Red		C-D
Pink		A-C

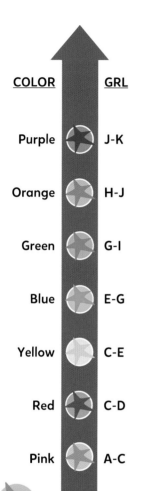

Leveled for Guided Reading

Early Bird Stories have been edited and leveled by leading educational consultants to correspond with guided reading levels. The levels are assigned by taking into account the content, language style, layout, and phonics used in each book.